For when they began to boast again,

"I've been through a tunnel and over a bridge. I've been through a town with a castle in the middle. I've been through a town with a church in the middle. I've been through a town with factories in the middle. I've even been to London town. I'm a MAIN LINE ENGINE and I've carried the King. My name is *Royal Red*. *By Special Appointment.* And now I'm quite happy on my own branch line. WHOOOEEEEEOOO."

And the *Royal Red* went happily to **sleep**.

minus. "This Little Red Engine is now a Main Line Engine. You must give it a name and paint it on its sides in gold. Call it *Royal Red*. And add *By Special Appointment*."

And they did as he said.

So when the Little Red Engine went home how happy and proud it was. For on its side in letters of gold was written *Royal Red, by Special Appointment to His Majesty The King.*

And when the two other big engines came back what was their surprise.

And as they drew into the platform, " WHOOOEEEOOO. I've been through a tunnel and over a bridge. I've been through a town with a castle in the middle. I've been through a town with a church in the middle. I've been through a town with factories in the middle. I'm a main line train and I'm carrying the King. And here I am in London town. Chufffffff." And the Little Red Engine pulled up at the platform.

When the King got out of his coach all the people came crowding around him. " Just a moment, please." And he waved them aside.

Then he walked up the platform to the Little Red Engine.

" I never thought you would do it," he said. " A very fine performance. You are not a moment late."

Then turning to the station master of the big London ter-

" What a funny little engine to be out on the main line, and pulling the King too, and it hasn't even a name!" And the suburban electric trains sniffed as they went past, but they really had no right to for they had no names either.

And all along the line were the backs of houses. Houses and houses and houses and houses. The Little Red Engine hadn't thought there could be so many in the world.

Then in they came to an *enormous* station. A dozen platforms? There were over twenty! And all the people, and porters and trucks and taxis! "Make way please, make way. Mind your backs. Ting Ting." And boys who shouted "Paper! Paper! Chocolates, papers, cigarettes!"

They came to a town with factories in the middle, and canals with barges and cranes and wharves and lorries.

" HEEEEEOOOOOOO," screamed the factory whistle. Clang clang clang clang, went the noise of the machines. Hoot toot, went the tugs on the canal.

" I've been through a tunnel and over a bridge. I've been through a town with a castle in the middle. I've been through a town with a church in the middle. I've been through a town with factories in the middle. I'm a main line train and I'm carrying the King. WHQOOEEEOOO."

And soon they came near London town. On every side were railway lines, and electric trains which hadn't even an engine were running past and looking at the Little Red Engine curiously.

They came to a town with a church in the middle. The bells were ringing, "Oh! All good people come to church. Oh! All good people come to church."

"I've been through a tunnel and over a bridge. I've been through a town with a castle in the middle. I've been through a town with a church in the middle. I'm a main line train and I'm carrying the King. WHOOOEEEOOO."

They came to a river, very wide and very deep. Over the river went a bridge. The very first bridge the Little Red Engine had come to.

Clack-a-tack-tack. Clack-a-tack-tack. Clack-a-tack-tack. And there they were on the other side of the river.

" I've been through a tunnel and over a bridge. I'm a main line train and I'm carrying the King. WHOOOEEEOOO," sang the Little Red Engine.

It came to a town, the first it had seen. In the middle was a castle and soldiers were drilling. Their band was playing and the gun went off Boom Boom !

" I've been through a tunnel and over a bridge. I've been through a town with a castle in the middle. I'm a main line train and I'm carrying the King, WHOOOEEEOOO."

And then they came to a tunnel, the first it had ever been through.   It took a deep breath :

WHOOOEEEEEOOOOO

" Burra wurra, burra wurra, burra wurra.

WHOOOEEEOOOO

And there they were out on the other side.

" I've been through a tunnel.   I'm a main line train and I'm carrying the King,

WHOOOOOOEEEEOOO

sang the Little Red Engine.

And in he got, with all his friends, and the whistle blew and away they went.

"I'm a main line train and I'm carrying the King.

And out it ran on the Great Main Line.

The storm of the day before was over now and the sun shone, and the sky was blue and the Little Red Engine went puffing along the line.

"I'm a main line train and I'm carrying the King.

And that was a bigger load than the Little Red Engine had ever pulled before.

" Are you sure you can do it?" asked the Station Master anxiously.

" Chuffa chuff chuff," cried the Little Red Engine. And its driver leant out of the cab.

" Don't you worry. The Little Red Engine can do it."

Then the King came along.

When he saw the Little Red Engine,

" Is this the best you can do?" he asked.

" I'm afraid it is, Your Majesty."

" Well, let's hope there will be no accidents."

LUGGAGE

FROM Taddlecombe Ju.

TO London

NAME H. M. the King

ADDRESS Buckingham Palace

in this. And behind this coach were seven first-class carriages and all the King's friends were going to ride in these. And behind that again were ten big luggage vans, and all the King's luggage would hardly go in these.

So they fixed a special coach to the Little Red Engine, newly
painted with the King's arms upon it, and the King would ride

And the Station Master shook his head, but as he did so he heard a little whistle from the engine shed.

"Wait a minute," he said. And ran to look inside.

There he saw the Little Red Engine, its face shining.

"Chuffa chuff chuff. Chuffa chuff chuff. Let me go. I can do it. Let me go. I really can."

"Well, the Great Main Line is a difficult business. Are you sure you could manage? You've never had main line experience." And the Station Master stood in doubt.

"Chuffa chuff chuff. I'm sure I can."

And the Little Red Engine looked so eager.

"We can but try," said the Station Master. And he ran and told the King's messengers he thought he could manage something.

But what a misfortune!

For the King himself was staying near Taddlecombe Junction. And he had to get home by the very next day.

"Matters of State. Matters of State. Very Important."

And here were the main line engines useless for three days more.

So the King sent messengers to the Station Master.

"Come, sir, come. Surely you can think of something. Have you no other engine fit to do the work?"

And there it was stuck fast. And the snow fell and covered it up.
And the men who came to dig it out shook their heads and blew
on their fingers.

"We'll never get her out under three days at least."

And they sat down and drank cocoa to keep themselves
warm.

fell, and a tree was blown down and fell across the great main line to the South. And the Big Green Engine, *Beauty of the South,* went rushing right into it, dada-da-da, dada-da-da, dada-da-da BOOM! And jumped the line and over it fell, and the wheels went whrrrrrr, and the steam went whooooshhhhh, and though nobody was hurt, there the engine lay, by the side of the track.

"It will take three days to move her," said the driver, scratching his head, and sat down on the lines to wait for help to come.

At the same time the Big Black Engine, *Pride o' the North,* went puffing through the storm, chuffa chuffa chuffa chuffff, chuffa chuffa chuffa chuffff, and the snow fell fast and it could not see and it did not know that a snowdrift had blocked the great main line to the North, and into the snowdrift it ran HOOOSH!

And the Little Red Engine would stay awake and think to itself,

"How lucky they are! I wish I could see the things that they have seen, I wish I could go through a tunnel, I wish I could run on a bridge. I like my branch line very much, and I shouldn't like to leave it. But if only once I could be a Main Line engine. Only once and then I should be content."

And it would let off steam in such a sigh, Whooooeeeee, and would go to sleep and would dream of the Great Main Line.

Now one day in the winter there was an awful storm. The wind blew, the snow and some are small, but a hundred of your villages would hardly fill one street! And some have castles and some fine churches, and some are full of factories and dockyards and warehouses. And as for the stations! Why, the least have a dozen plat-forms."

And the Little Red Engine could only sigh with envy, because how could it tell when the others were exaggerating?

"And as for the tunnels," they would say, "Whooooo, there *is* a thrill. You take a deep breath, WHEEEOOOOO, Wurra Burra, Wurra Burra, Wurra Burra, Whoooeeeooo; and there you are out on the other side. And as for the bridges, Clack-a-tack, Clack-a-tack, Clack-a-tack till you're over. Give us the main line," they said, and sighed contentedly before they went to sleep.

The Big Black Engine was called *Pride o' the North,* written in letters of gold on its side, and the Big Green Engine was called *Beauty of the South*; but the Little Red Engine had no name at all, only a number written in black, 394, for it only worked on a branch line, and the others were Main Line engines.

How sad was the Little Red Engine! Every night when it got home from its run it heard the other engines boasting of what they had seen.

" Ah ! ", they would say, " You don't know what you are missing. All you ever see are empty fields and cows and a village here and there, and your only excitements are your ten level crossings and everyone knows that they are out of date.

" You should just see what we see every day of our lives ! Towns, towns. Can you even imagine a town ? Some are big

Once upon a time there was a Little Red Engine. It lived in a shed with a Big Black Engine and a Big Green Engine at the junction of Taddlecombe, where the great main line to the North, and the great main line to the South met the little branch line on which the Little Red Engine was running.

THE LITTLE RED ENGINE
GETS A NAME

story by
DIANA ROSS

[Denney, Diana]

pictures by
LEWITT-HIM

———————

For John Scott

FABER AND FABER LIMITED LONDON